Unraveling

Poetry from the Soul

Sidney Kitt

Unraveling

Poetry from the Soul

Sidney Kitt

Written by Sidney Kitt

Illustrated by Sherman Powell

"There is no greater agony than bearing
an untold story inside you"

- Maya Angelou

To the many souls

Who have brought me along

The journey of love

Pain

And everything In-

Between.

Table of Contents

Part 1:

Loving

My eyes told you

"Hello",

And my compassion

gave you entrance

Soft touch and poetic words entrap me

I want this new experience to last

You are the hightide of my enquiry

Methinks my heart beats much too fast

We crave that passionate love

That soulful,

That unconditional love

Which a higher power has already introduced to us

We go around in circles as the world turns

And the years go by

And I only lose when I lock my feelings

Behind closed doors

And you only lose when you run behind

Brick walls from the truth,

That God could have possibly given me you

Let me go under the tip of the iceberg

No matter how cold and dark it may get

Icy waters laced with trauma and regret

I hope I never become one of your

regrets

You on My mind,

Is slowly starting to happen

All the time

I trust you enough

To turn towards you

Both during times of weakness

And times of strength

Whether graceful

Or a fucking mess

But still,

You love me regardless

I never knew

I was capable of

Continuously missing one being

For what feels like

A

lifetime

Our fingers

And legs

Were tangled

In ways

That made me believe

We were always one

You open my third eye,

While releasing sweet juices from between my thighs

I am captured by your smile,

And those brown eyes entrap me

Every time

I climax,

Mentally,

From the way your intellect binds me

Holding me physically captive,

You captivate me,

Your essence essentially causing raptures inside of me

The silence of your lips speaks quietly

You took my hand and grabbed my soul

Out of my body

Astral projecting

To mingle with yours across spatial galaxies

I cannot see

A meaning without you here with me

But only past, present, and future lives

Where we are meant to be

His lips whispered secrets,

That my heart so desperately wanted to hear

Baby,

I just need you to speak a little louder

Let me breathe positive affirmations in your ear

When your demons get too loud

I am nothing more than

An artist

Attempting to understand you

The way I exhale my poetry

With your head laying gently upon my breast and my hand

against your heartbeat, we will have the strength to compete

against what they say on the Main Street. Our love will be

elite, upbeat, thick heat, sun-sweet; oh yes. It will be...

Sweet honeydew

Fueling me with natural sugar

He anointed my melancholy away

With his exotic universe

Encompassed in unknown wisdom

He gave me bits and pieces of the treasure

Which is him

He caught my attention

Like a forbidden book

On a vast library shelf

Arousing me to open up

His pages

So as not to assume

From an elegant cover

I

Found

The

Hidden

Parts

Of

Myself

Within

You

Within book pages

And the lullabies of 90's Love songs

I only see your outstretched hand

Tempting me behind it all

It was a Fall day, after school

When we took our leisurely walk up the hill

Music from Jhené Aiko blasting from the speakers

My voice captured you like the scent of flowers

So, you picked a red one for me

Out of a stranger's backyard

For you had no money

So, I cherished that flower

Pressed within the pages of the

"Twilight" novel by Stephenie Meyer

May neither of the two,

Either it or you

Wither away

In the process of

Giving you a part of myself

I continue to observe you

With calmness,

Mindfulness,

And a pure heart

Part 2:

Doubting

I want to be wrapped up inside your body

Heat

Feeling your heart

Beat

Beside me

Without having to rely on myself,

And this warm soul

Yet cold sheets

My worst fear

Is to be abandoned

Disregarded

Used

So please don't leave

After I give you my all

Please promise to stay

After everyone already left

He sways my thoughts

In every direction, without my consent

Scrambling

And

Unscrambling

Do not mistake, I am a once in a lifetime opportunity

And my lips utter once in a lifetime promises

Show me that you are in fact a reality

Prove that you will not leave,

Once you receive all of me

Heart broken

Save me from cardiac arrest

You are heart spoken

You clean up this heap of a mess

That my melancholy makes

I warn you not to destroy it once more

It is hard to not be needy when it comes to you

But then I realize I am not yours to begin with

I may not even have that right

I barely made the cut to be your maybe

But from the start, you were my always

A candle

                    Flickers

The taste of your essence

                        Enters

My heart is

                          Confused.

When I create scenarios

In my favor,

A dose of positivity from my own self

Scenarios of you

My intuition softly asks me:

"Is this person,

Truly healthy for your

Well- being?"

What

    makes

        You

            forget

                About

                    a

                        Gift is,

                        It

                    does

                Not

            come

        To

    you

At

    the Right Time

Part 3:

Breaking

You force yourself

To hold him within you

Until your mouth bleeds

And your eyes burn

Pushing away your thoughts

To please him

Knowing that

He will never be pleased

My womb breaks,

Only blood pours out instead

Do not give him the satisfaction,

Of knowing just how much the wound bleeds

I remember when my body refused my first

And my mind went on lockdown

All to please him out of desperation

Because I thought real true love was a myth

I forced myself to settle for less

Because of a self esteem that was less than average

And all the boys and that influential man in the past,

That treated me less than my worth

Your fear of saying no

Continued

Even within

His bedroom

So, your body decided

To answer for you

Scrunch your eyelids shut

Until yellow spots appear

If you pretend not to see it

The fear may go away

You were naïve

Expecting to see him for

Intellectual stimulation and affection

But he only wanted one thing,

The extra stuff was a game

He throws the heavy weight

Of his body

On top of you

Suffocated

You know what he is about to do

Your mouth cannot speak the word "NO!"

...but you do not say yes

Instead you stay frozen

And take It

Fear, discomfort, and pain

It cannot fit

It cannot fit

So, he forces it to... continuously

You have become numb as you physically shut down

Unmoving

He is annoyed now, sexually frustrated

He awkwardly bends your body

This way and that

Your mind cannot react,

As he tries to force it to fit

He gives up,

And makes you give him head instead

You feel like a whore...but you do it anyway

You fear saying no

You fear what he may be capable of

You fear him leaving so you do it anyway

Despite the dread within.

It was only 3 years later,

When you realize from the words of a friend

That pain,

The event that you experienced

Was Sexual Assault.

Part 4:

Ending

I used to look at you with fondness in my eyes

They all noticed except for you

Since I never held your attention

Long enough for you to pay attention

So, this heart is no longer for you

(Every day I fight against myself,

To save myself

And my sanity)

They say happiness is found from within

But what do you do,

If all you find is overthinking and fear of

The unknown

When your heart is no longer your home

Because it cannot be trusted,

And your mind still cannot figure out

How to correspond with your soul

She wrote in her mystical diary

Since humans were too scary to trust

I held down the vomit

I went with the flow

I put on a show

I pushed my life aside to try and help yours

While you did nothing

Now I struggle to remember who I am

Depressed over a man who only loved me partly

Cutting him off was the best decision made

He only loved his bed and his music, he was not sorry

I spent over 5 years wishing for what he never gave

You left me numb

You left me hurting

You left me trying to put together the pieces

Of a puzzle that only gets destroyed in the process

I loved you

Who did not love me

But it was still a love more

Than I had loved myself

Drinking to numb the pain

Wiping away the unshed tears

A storm is wading

While my heart ripped apart

Leaving a void of emptiness

Her father sarcastically asked her,

"What boy would give you flowers?"

He laughed at her self-confident poetry

He threatened her for speaking back

The boy at school,

Called her ugly for a year

He felt her up on the bus in 8th grade

She wore long skirts to cover the shape of her ass

But still she got groped anyway

Her mom told her not to be so weak and naïve

Every boy broke her, or was broken

Her brother,

Never allowed himself to grow close to her

Everyone saw her flaws and acne scars

Her first love never loved her

He traumatized her, in every sense of the word

She lost herself in the chaos and cried

To them, her tears meant nothing

For her, it was the begging for happiness

Good job

You have finally realized

The toxic relationship

With the man you call father

Led to nothing but

The subconscious crave for

Emotionally unavailable men

They all break your heart just the same

Part 5:

Forgiving

I peered out the window at the moon,

And finally allowed myself to think of you

To be in love with the ideology of love

To crave love from everyone else

Except myself

Should be a sin

Since it causes hurt

And pain

With every step of the way

I turn the other cheek

And continue down the same road

When it would be easier to become steel

Menacing and cold

I seem to fall for danger

Toxic soul ties and vacant eyes

Troublesome hearts worse than my own

What is stopping me

From creating my own sense of home

Why do I still fear the thought of being alone?

I break down and cry

Because even when I do receive love

It is by those still in pain

And I feel my own self slipping away

When I always give more love than people seem to take

My overthinking

Shakes me from my slumber

Of memories

That I wish went differently

There goes my first love

Who will never come back

I cry yet smile

But he cannot see my tears

They have already dried

I have no more left to give

I start loving myself

It is a foreign,

A foreign feeling

Pain

Trickles under your skin

Like the sharp tools inflaming your gums

Which the dentist used on you

Pain

Caressed your heart with rusty chains

When you were always chosen last place

By gym teachers and men alike

Underneath your folds it ceases you

As stretchmarks creep up your sides

Another loved one has died

Pain

Leaving a dull pressure in your head

As tears trickle out from eyelid corners

At fear of the unknown

Pain

But I thank you,

Pain

For finding your way to me

So that I can know of Love

Delicate flower

You are soft and pure

You lie to yourself

You lie to make others happy

Delicate flower

You are underwatered

Your roots were ripped away from you

Emotional trauma blossoms from within your petals

Delicate flower

You bare seeds to the world

Which the wind refuses to spread

Delicate flower

You always need to be nourished

Before these humans trample you

The pain you caused

Still lingers in the corners

Ever so faintly

But I can never tell you the trauma you caused

Since my trustfulness and self-esteem,

Were also to blame

And you were never the victim

You are out there living your best life

So, I will push this all behind

And try my best to live mine

Human

You are insignificant compared to

The vastness of the cosmos

Until you realize that You Are the Universe

Experiencing itself

Hang in there

And embrace the bumpy ride

To gain back Consciousness

Finish that homework assignment. Read that book that has been collecting dust on your shelf. Write that poem. Create that masterpiece. Light those candles. Practice your meditation. Drink your water. Read that scripture. Pray when needed. Control your emotions. Limit your speaking. Be more optimistic. Clear your mind. Replenish your soul.

Learn to put yourself first, instead of giving control to those who will not plan to stay.

It is a weird,

Yet liberating feeling

To not like

Or be in love with

Anyone but

Yourself.

She was a weird soul encompassed within a mass of flesh

She quested for the truth

And lived her life being in love

She went from broken to found,

Because she had found herself

The lesson of pain

Is to Heal

I am learning to love, without

Too much attachment

With patience and mindfulness

It can be so easy

One that transcends selfishness

With no expectations

Only gratitude

Its so easy to love yourself

When you begin to put in the work

I dream and write poetry

To feel my own essence beside me

As birds sing melodies outside my window

And my heart pangs relentlessly

I wonder if these dreams of mine

Will one day be a reality

They love the dimples in my smile

My soft ways and old style

My eloquence and grace,

That I carry from place to place

It is the swaying hips within my walk

The intelligence within my voice as I talk

Kindheartedness and expertise

Love and affection flowing with ease

I sit silently,

Full of Maya Angelou poems

The sun beats down, while cool breeze lifts me up

Her pages of words turn,

Then start anew

I feel her in my spirit,

Taste her poetry on my tongue

Reminisce of her wise talk in my dreams

Following the seams leading to infinity

Her soul is hidden under the bellies of singing birds,

The *Cage bird sings* because its free

Still she rises through the clouds,

A *phenomenal woman* shining through the *Greyday*

She is the *passing time*,

Mourning grace

She left the earth where she belongs,

Where we belong, A Duet

Maya Angelou was a *freedom fighter* through her pen

Fancier than a *'Time-Square-Shoeshine-Composition'*

When I go to heaven,

Is when she *Come to me*

Maya Angelou is still *working on white liberal*s

And I give her no *Refusal*

Poetry

Flows

Silently

Loudly

Consistently

Constantly

Wildly

From

The

Depths

Of

My

Soul

Holed In

You wonder what your life purpose is

It might be as little as

The positive energy you exude when in front of me

Your therapeutic laughter and

Words of encouragement

Your nurturing ways

And knowledge that home is where the heart is

Now is the time

Holed away in our houses

Where we find out where our heart is

I may not be the next Maya Angelou,

But still, like dust, I rise...

To the brinks of history

With my uniqueness and creativity

And will find a way to become a person,

That I will be proud of

Words cannot express

The light that I have acquired

The slight spring in my step

And the blessings I am given

I worry too often

About what the future holds

Asking questions that

I cannot possibly know the answer to

Until the future has become the present moment,

Will I reach my goal?

I know at times, the inner me, she hurts

But surviving another day
With her head held high
Is what makes her strong

A constant reason for admiration

So, I will try my best
To do the same
For every aspect of myself

Do not follow others

Only to lose yourself,

When you can just

Create your own path

Strip away the mask

Strip away the pain that escalates from your ego

You have felt trapped,

Mentally enslaved

For too long

You want to go home

Nonphysical

You have no clue, where it might reside

You now know,

That authentic happiness only arrives

When you finally begin to conquer the mind

We have a long way to go my friend

My energy is sacred,

I do not live this life for you

But only for me

I have a soul, therefore allow me to be free

I do not need to do as you do

I just need to focus on me

Acting patiently, I say grace then meditate

Begging my flesh to reciprocate with my spirit

Guided growth,

I am a seed planted that takes root into the earth

And generally, grows greener

Gaining generosity

Granting graceful gardens

Think of the hugs

     You give others as

          Silent hugs to yourself

               We are all just reflections of

          One another

     And we are all deserving

Of love.

To my past self

The hurt you go through

Will become

The lessons you needed

To grow

And to my future

I cannot wait

To see what is in store

People may bury their noses in books,

Plug their ears with music

Break their hands through writing stories

All as a form of escape

Take drugs to wash away

The remembrance of their name

Self- harm to wash away the

Mental and emotional pain

Meditate even,

To spiritually drift away

And learning that self- love

Is the best form of love,

Unconditional love

Is the only way we can truly

Fight to see another day

Positivity

From

Within

Speaks

Volumes

There is cosmic energy

Between the legs of a woman

That could change

A person's life

With the strength

To bring new life

Into the world

It muddles the brainwaves

Of those who cannot perceive

The power it truly holds

It is orgasmic

It is intuitive

Of what it allows entrance

The vagina. Yoni. Pussy.

Is what makes the female gender,

Almost Godly

Use is Wisely

Watching my mirror reflection

It is a reminder

That I exist

That I am not only alive,

But loved

And will always be here to stay

Princess fairytales of deprived women

Needing a man to swoop in to save them

Portrayal of a damsel in distress,

Should no longer be normalized

For we do not need anyone,

Without first needing ourselves

A man

Cannot scrub all your personal baggage away

Normalize

Implemented boundaries and discovery of your own body

Do not let anyone force you into

Something you never wanted

Just to make them happy

Normalize the gift of self

Learning and loving of self

Normalize masturbation for women

As much as men confidently brag about it

Normalize makeup and surgeries and natural beauty

Overstanding the knowledge of soul,

Over what you look like

Or what lays between your legs

Normalize the heartbreak and pain of women

Because we all can gain

Self-appreciation in the end

Sometimes all we need

Is a close friend

A therapist

Patient family member

Or willing stranger

To vent to

Do something that you will be passionate about

for the rest of your days.

About the Author

Sidney Kitt is a woman of awkward moments yet poetic words. A lover of music, emotional romance novels, authenticity, and vulnerability. Her first name, Sandra, meaning "defender of mankind", is the life purpose she strives to achieve. She is a college student, worker, daughter, younger sister, goofball, and best friend. Her role models are her mother, Maya Angelou, and the Universe.

****

I am a human being that goes through love, laughter, and heartbreak. Who experiences tears, trauma, and suffering. A woman who holds a tattoo on her right arm which states: "Still I Rise"; a constant reminder to keep my head held high. I am simply another version of all of you, as we all reside in this Universe together.

Most importantly, I am a writer, who's deepest desire since the age of thirteen, was to one day share what I love most with all of you.

Acknowledgments

I am grateful towards every soul who influenced the creation and publication of this book, my first novel in the making. Specifically, I would like to thank my Mom, who genuinely appreciated the process within all my written works since age eleven and prior. No matter how well poised or rudimentary they were, she allowed me to have the novels and creative space needed for me to grow into becoming myself. I am thankful for my brother, Jerome, for encouraging me to consider publishing. Samantha, for her unwavering support and editing skills. And Sherman, for helping with illustration and design.

I am also thankful for Ms. Lauren, Benjamin, Justen, Isis, Nasir, Rozelyn, Aarionna, and Tydahja, as well as every other inspirational person who has guided and supported me along this journey in some way or another. And to my first love and those who brought me pain, who treated me less than my worth, I thank you for the hurt that only led to growth, and the unraveling of this book.

And thank you, to my fellow readers, for walking this path along with me to our destination- the end of this book.

I sincerely love you all.

To My Beautiful Reader

Dear reader,

You have now reached the end of this vast exploration: the closing of my first book. I hope you enjoyed indulging within the five stages of my personal experiences, my poetry from the soul. Through this story which covered the trials and tribulations of loving, learning, trauma, forgiveness, and healing, I hope you were able to relate along the way.

Life, including romantic relationships, may not always go as planned, but we have the right to choose to love ourselves despite what we may endure. Self-love always wins.

If you wish to connect or read more of my works, you can find me at:

Instagram.com/unveiledpoet

SandraKitt1998@gmail.com

Made in the USA
Middletown, DE
27 November 2020